F

Herobrine's Quest – Book No. 4

by Steve DeWinter

Disclaimer:

Any use of copyrightable elements, trademarks and other intellectual property associated with the Minecraft brand video game is done simply for descriptive purposes only, and such description does not indicate any endorsement by or affiliation with the owner(s) of this game.

Summary

As Josh, Andre, and Suzy are about to enter the town of Silverrock, they meet their first dragon and discover secrets that they never expected to find.

Do you want the author of this book to visit your classroom?

Ask your teacher to contact Steve DeWinter at writer@stevedw.com to discuss having an author visit with your class using the power of the internet and a webcam.

Watch Steve and his son, the real Josh who inspired the Josh in this story, play games and have fun together on their YouTube Channel.

https://www.youtube.com/c/odnttv

Ramblin' Prose Publishing

Copyright © 2015 Steve DeWinter

HEROBRINE'S QUEST is a trademark of Ramblin' Prose Publishing.

eBook Edition

ISBN-10: 1-61978-118-2

ISBN-13: 978-1-61978-118-4

Paperback Edition

ISBN-10: 1-61978-119-0

ISBN-13: 978-1-61978-119-1

Chapter 1

Andre kicked a small rock. It rolled ahead of him, and then back toward him, gaining speed as it rolled down the hill. It was amazing how real everything seemed.

He, his twin brother Josh, and Suzy, one of their most annoying classmates from school, had traveled to this computer generated world to stop Herobrine, an artificial intelligence whose sole purpose was to defeat humanity.

But so far after leaving Estermead, all they had accomplished was walking from one hill to another stopping only to sleep. Every time they crested a hill, all he saw before them were more hills.

Suzy had named herself leader of their little group, and now, for some reason, she was leading them to the peak of the highest hill in the area. The rock had rolled all the way back to him and he kicked it up the hill again. "Tell me again why we are walking?"

He looked at Suzy and sneered. "Oh, that's right. You sold our horses for..." He looked at Josh. "What were they called?"

"Cubits," Josh answered as he hunched over and half-walked half-climbed the hill in front of him.

Andre shook his head. "Right. Cubits. Hah! What a ripoff."

Suzy gave him a hard stare. "We needed the

money. How do you think we paid for the inn we slept in last night? With your good looks?"

Andre shrugged his shoulders. "We could have tried."

She shook her head. "We don't need horses. But we do need money."

Andre held his arms wide, indicating the steep hill they were walking up. "I get why we didn't need the horses, but why didn't we take the road that went along the river? Nooooo! You wanted to climb the tallest mountain you could find."

Suzy pushed past him and climbed faster. "We're almost there."

Andre rushed to keep up with her. "And

what are we going to find when we get to the top?"

She paused at the peak of the hill and looked around at the valley below. Andre joined her and she pointed down. "This."

Andre looked out over the valley. "I don't see anything."

Suzy smiled. "Precisely. According to the map, this valley is called Dragon's Run. There are no towns, no farms, no houses, and no people."

"You dragged me all the way up a mountain to show me nothing?"

Josh caught up with them and set his pack down at his feet.

Suzy shook her head and opened her arms wide, indicating the whole valley below. "No, silly. I dragged you up here so you can learn how to fly."

Josh's heart caught in his throat. "Fly?"

Suzy nodded. "Nobody will see us in this valley. It's the perfect place."

Josh looked out over the edge of the cliff. The valley below was a long way down. "Why did we need to come all the way up here to learn how to fly?"

Suzy shuffled close to the edge and peered down. "Call it incentive."

She turned and looked at Andre. "Who wants to go first?"

Andre waved his hand with a flourish as he bowed. "Ladies first."

She shook her head. "I think you should go first, since you want to fly so bad."

Andre puffed up his chest. "Oh, I'll go first. No problem. I was just being a gentleman."

Suzy laughed loudly, her cackles echoing off the taller mountains on the other side of the valley. "You? A gentleman? Please!"

Andre crossed his arms. "You want me to go first?"

She nodded, a huge smile on her face.

Andre looked out over the cliff and took a half step back. "Fine. I'll go first."

He walked away from the edge of the cliff.

"Where are you going?" Suzy asked.

Andre stopped several feet away and turned around. "Getting a running head start."

Suzy and Josh watched as Andre bounced up and down on his feet.

Suzy egged him on. "Anytime hero."

Andre stopped bouncing. "I'm just getting ready."

Suzy crossed her arms. "What's to get ready for? You jump off, you fly."

"You make it sound so easy."

"And you're making it needlessly hard."

Andre crouched into a runner's starting position, his hands in front of him and his legs bent slightly.

Suzy laughed. "This isn't the Olympics."

"Quiet," he hissed.

He took several quick breaths, letting them out just as quickly.

"Here I go... I'm going now... On three..."

Suzy stamped her foot. "Just go!"

Andre sprang forward and shot out over the edge of the cliff.

He hung in the air for a brief moment, and then dropped like a rock, screaming the whole way down until he disappeared into the trees below.

Suzy looked over at Josh. "Nobody ever makes the first jump."

Josh peered out over the edge. "How do we go get him?"

She pointed to a path that went down the side of the hill and into the valley below. "We walk."

Josh sighed. "Yay, more walking."

Suzy motioned to the edge of the cliff. "You can always take Andre's shortcut."

Josh half-smiled. "No thanks, I'll walk."

Chapter 2

When Suzy and Josh found Andre two hours later, he was sitting on a large rock by a river that ran through the middle of the valley.

He looked over at Suzy. "Did you know I would fall?"

She laughed. "I had a pretty good idea."

He stood up and winced, clearly in pain. "I broke both my legs you know."

She looked him over as he stretched slowly. "You look fine now."

"Oh sure, now. But it still hurt."

"Quit being a baby. I knew you wouldn't die. I mean, look at Josh. He survived a direct explosion from a Creeper."

Andre looked at Josh who shrugged his shoulders with a smile.

Andre looked back at Suzy and limped away from the rock. "Well, from now on, I'll take my flying lessons from someone who really knows how to fly."

Suzy put her hands on her hips. "Oh yeah? Who else are you going to find in this world who can fly?"

Andre pointed to the sky. "How about that?"

Suzy and Josh looked to where Andre pointed and saw the biggest dragon they had ever seen... no, the only dragon they had ever seen, clinging to the side of the highest peak of the mountain on the other side of the valley.

Its skin was black as coal and the eyes reflected back the sunlight like glowing orbs.

It spread its dark leathery wings and took off into the air. They watched as it wheeled around the valley, catching rising air currents along the edge. It reacted suddenly, as if it had heard something among the forest below, and flew down out of sight.

Suzy turned to Andre. "If you can convince that thing to teach you how to fly without eating you first, I'd be your servant for a month."

Andre smirked. "My servant, eh?"

Josh reached out and helped Andre walk across the rocks along the river's edge. "Don't listen to her, Andre, we'll figure it out."

"No, no," Andre replied. "I like her proposal." He looked out into the forest in the direction the dragon had landed. "Let's go find that dragon and see what happens."

Chapter 3

On a farm twenty miles north of Dragon's Run Valley, Larissa stood up and wiped the sweat from her brow. She tilted the basket in her hands and watched the ripe strawberries roll around inside. She had been picking them from the rows of plants on her father's farm for several hours, and still the basket was only half full.

The summer had been a cold one, and the strawberry fields were not as plentiful as they had been in years past. Unless she could fill twenty baskets before the harvest festival next week, they would not have enough to barter for the supplies they needed.

She rolled the strawberries around in the basket. They were also smaller and darker than past crops. This was going to be a rough winter.

A bird's hunting call echoed across the sky. It was louder than the call of the hawks that searched for mice in her father's fields. Maybe an eagle had made its way farther south this year, to escape the colder temperatures.

She scanned the sky and froze.

A dragon was dropping down out of the bright blue sky straight toward her.

She dropped the basket of strawberries and ran for the house. As she ran, the dragon's shadow spread out around her. It was getting bigger as the dragon was getting closer.

She could feel the sudden rush of air as the dragon beat its wings against the still air, slowing itself down as it neared the ground.

Just as she reached the edge of the field a three toed claw wrapped around her whole body and lifted her, her feet dangling helplessly above the ground.

She let out a blood curdling scream and her father rushed out of the small cottage.

Their eyes connected as the dragon carried her up and over the roof of their home. He watched in shock as a dragon flew away with his only daughter.

Chapter 4

Andre kicked at another rock on the side of the road. Josh was reading the map and checked their position against the sun. He folded the map and tucked it into his bag. "We should reach Silverrock before nightfall."

Andre half-laughed. "Good. I'm sick of sleeping on the ground."

Suzy looked over at him from where she sat on a big rock. "I keep telling you, we don't need to sleep."

Josh closed the flap on his bag. "Yeah, but the last time we tried walking around at night, we ended up going in circles. And I still can fall asleep, so why not?"

Suzy stood up. "True. That's why I didn't complain when we decided to stop and camp each night. But I must admit, it will be nice to lie down on a real bed inside a room with walls and a ceiling."

They heard the cry of a creature high up in the sky. They looked up and saw the large black dragon flying back toward the valley they had left hours before.

Josh squinted against the low sun. "Is that the same dragon?"

Andre held a hand up to shield his eyes. "It looks like it has something in its hand. What is that? A bear?"

Suzy held both hands up to shield the bright rays of the sun as the dragon flew overhead. "It's not a bear. It's a girl!"

Suzy started to run back toward the valley when Andre stepped in her path and stopped her. "Where do you think you're going?"

"We have to help her."

"Are you crazy? There's no way we can keep up with that dragon. And even if you could catch up to it, what were you planning to do?"

Suzy glared at him. "I don't know. But I can't just stand here and watch someone get eaten by a dragon."

Andre pointed to the dragon, which had

grown smaller as it got farther away. "Look, it's already halfway to the valley. We couldn't keep up with it even if we wanted to."

Suzy pushed Andre out of the way. "Speak for yourself."

She jumped into the air, but rather than falling back to the ground, she shot up into the sky and took off after the dragon.

Andre's mouth hung open.

He looked over at Josh. "Did you know she could fly?"

Josh shook his head without taking his eyes off of Suzy.

Andre looked back to the sky, and together, they watched Suzy rocket through the air after the dragon.

Chapter 5

Suzy felt the wind pulling at her cheeks as she flew even faster to catch up with the dragon. She enjoyed the rush of wind through her hair, and the feeling of absolute freedom. When those two fools, Andre and Josh, had decided to sleep the night away, she had taken that time to learn how to fly. And now, it was going to come in handy.

Ahead of her, the dragon swooped down into the valley beyond the mountains. She pushed herself to go faster. From what little she knew about dragons, which was nothing really, since they didn't exist in the real world, she could only guess what would happen as soon as the dragon landed. If it was anything like a normal bird of prey, as soon as it touched down, it would kill and eat whatever it had captured in its claws.

She couldn't let that happen, because this dragon's intended meal was a person.

The air was thinner, and colder, along the top of the mountain range, but she pushed herself to keep flying. As she crested the top of the mountain, she saw the dragon swoop in low over the valley floor and disappear into the trees of the forest below.

She tucked her arms in tight against her body and let herself drop, letting gravity assist her in gaining speed. She had to get to that dragon before that poor girl was dinner.

She spread her arms out wide and angled herself to fly over the forest. She scanned through the tops of the trees, looking for any sign of them.

She spotted a large black shape on the ground as she flew past a clearing in the forest. She quickly circled around and slowed for a better look.

In the middle of the clearing was the dragon on its back, a large arrow sticking out of its chest just under the front left leg.

She dropped down into the forest and approached the clearing on foot.

As she reached the open area, she heard a man's voice.

"Are you okay mademoiselle?"

She peeked around a tree and saw a man reaching down to a young woman lying on the ground. The woman took the man's offered hand and stood up. "I think so. What happened?"

"I was about to set up camp when I saw this vile beast come over the top of the mountain. When I saw that he had a beautiful creature in his devil-like claws, I drew my longbow and waited for him at the edge of the forest."

The woman blushed at the mention of the

word beautiful. "Who are you?"

The man removed his feathered hat and bowed with a flourish.

"The name's Dylan, dragon hunter extraordinaire, at your service."

He stood back up and replaced his hat. "And who did I have the honor of saving today?"

She blushed again. "My name is Larissa."

He took her hand and kissed it. Suzy stuck her finger in her mouth, and mimicked throwing up. She had had enough of this and stepped out from behind the tree.

"Excuse me?"

Dylan and Larissa turned toward her. Dylan

looked startled at the sudden intruder. "Who are you?"

"My name is Suzy." She put her hand behind her back so he wouldn't be tempted to try and slobber all over it.

Dylan squinted at her. "What are you doing out here all alone, this far from a town?"

"I'm not alone. My friends and I are headed to Silverrock and took the shortcut through the valley."

Dylan approached her. "Your friends? Where are your parents?"

Suzy stuck her chin out defiantly. "It is just me and my friends."

Dylan shook his head, as if he were

admonishing a small child, which apparently, he thought he was. "That is very dangerous."

He suddenly stiffened and cocked his head to the side, as if a thought had just occurred to him. "How long were you hiding in there? What did you see?"

"To be honest, I kind of missed everything. I got here just as you were helping Larissa up." Suzy looked over at the dragon lying on its back in the middle of the clearing. "You really killed it with a single arrow?"

Dylan visibly relaxed and smiled. "That I did."

She looked again at the placement of the arrow. It was tucked in along the dragon's side under his front leg. From the angle it protruded out from the body, it didn't look like it had pierced the heart, lungs, or anything vital. It looked more like a grazing shot at best and should never have brought down an entire dragon.

Dylan placed a hand on her shoulder and turned her away from the dead dragon. "It's best not to look at death so closely, child."

He scanned the skies around him. "Besides, we should be going. Where there is one dragon, there are most certainly more."

He looked at Larissa. "Which way to your village?"

She checked the angle of the sun and

pointed. "I live that way."

Dylan smiled and crooked his arm out toward her. "Let's get you back home safe. I'm sure your family is very worried about you."

She looped her arm through his and smiled back. "It is just me and my father. He will be so happy when he finds out that you saved my life. There will be no way for him to repay you for your bravery."

Dylan smiled wider. "I'm sure we can come up with something."

Chapter 6

Andre ran as fast as he could and vaulted himself into the air. He fell unceremoniously back to the ground after only jumping less than a foot high. He shook his head and looked at Josh. "How did she do that?"

Josh pointed at three figures walking down the road toward them from the direction Suzy had followed the dragon. "Ask her yourself."

Andre squinted into the distance and saw Suzy walking with two adults. One of them looked like the girl who had been caught in the dragon's claw. The other looked like some kind of hunter. He had animal skins sewn together into a patchwork cloak that made him look like... well, like a hunter.

Andre sat down on the large rock next to Josh. "I can't ask her in front of people. Who are they? And why didn't she fly back?"

Josh shook his head. "I don't know."

Suzy spotted them and ran forward to meet them. "Hey guys."

Andre grabbed her arm and pulled her to the side of the road. "Who are they?"

She pulled her arm out of his hand and walked back over to the man and woman as they approached. "Guys, this is Dylan and Larissa. Dylan and Larissa, these are my friends Josh and Andre."

Dylan stuck his hand out. "Gentlemen, I'm pleased to meet your acquaintances."

Josh and Andre each shook his hand.

"Nice to meet you too," Josh replied.

"What are you?" Andre asked.

"Andre!" Suzy hissed.

Dylan laughed. "It's a valid question. I am a dragon hunter. And it was my good fortune to have noticed this young lady caught in the claws of certain death before it was too late."

Larissa blushed. "It was my good fortune that Dylan was around."

Dylan looked at the setting sun. "We should get going. It will be dark soon and we should get inside should there be any backlash from the dragon I killed earlier."

Andre's brow furrowed. "Backlash?"

Dylan smiled at him. "The other dragons might go looking for revenge for their fallen brother."

Andre's eyes enlarged. "Oh, right."

Larissa pointed down the road. "My father's farm is just over the next rise. We will get there just as the sun sets if we walk quickly."

Dylan crooked his arm for Larissa. "Then swift is what we shall be."

She took his arm and together they continued down the road.

Larissa looked at the small group. "You are

also welcome to spend the night at my house, what with dragons flying around looking for victims."

Andre nodded. "She's got a point. "

He ran up to join the couple as they walked down the road.

Suzy grabbed Josh's arm before he ran forward and held him back.

"I don't like this Dylan fellow. He rubs me the wrong way."

Josh laughed. "Why, because he saved that girl's life before you could? By the way, we still need to talk about how you know how to fly."

She let go of his arm and walked ahead of

him. "Later."

Josh ran to catch up to them as they all headed for Larissa's home.

Chapter 7

Larissa led them to a small cottage along the edge of a field. Dylan looked around when she ran for the door, calling out to her father.

Her father came running out, picked her up and spun her around. She whispered to him and he looked over at Dylan. He ran over, tears in his eyes, and knelt at Dylan's feet. He snatched up Dylan's hand and began kissing it. Dylan pulled his hand out of the man's iron grip and, grabbing his shoulders, stood him back up again.

He smiled at the old farmer. "So you are a simple farmer, huh?"

The man beamed with pride as he waved toward the strawberry fields around his small cottage. "My family has been picking the juiciest and most colorful strawberries for generations." The man's face drooped and the smile faded. "This season does not look to be our best."

Dylan looked disappointed. "I see."

Larissa's father took a deep breath and smiled again. He grabbed Dylan's arm and pulled him toward the cottage. "Come. We must celebrate Larissa's safe return thanks to you."

Larissa's father was so happy that his daughter was alive, he slaughtered their only sheep to make an elegant feast in honor of the brave dragon hunter. Dylan tried to refuse, but the farmer wouldn't hear of it and used up just about everything he had in the house for this single meal.

Josh, Andre, and Suzy couldn't refuse to join in the meal, but they took as little as possible. This man had so little to begin with, and they really didn't need to eat, so they didn't want to take much from him.

Dylan laughed and regaled everyone of his dragon hunting exploits. He had been saving towns and beautiful maidens from dragons for most of his adult life. He had come to this area because a fortune teller told him that

Silverrock was about to be besieged by dragons.

He tore another chunk of meat off of the mutton chop and popped it into his mouth. "I'm beginning to wonder if my actions today, saving the fair Larissa, might all be part of the prophecy told to me. I fear that the dragons are now going to attack Silverrock because of the dragon I killed in the forest."

Larissa's father pushed more food in front of Dylan. "Nonsense. Because of you, there is one less dragon to threaten Silverrock. You should have no problem defending the city."

Dylan wiped his mouth on a cloth and pushed his chair back. "That reminds me, I should be going. I have a lot of things to do if I am to be ready to fight dragons at Silverrock."

Everyone stood up at the same time. Larissa grabbed his arm. "Please stay."

Her father rushed to Dylan's other side and also grabbed an arm. "Yes. Stay until you are full and well rested."

Dylan shook his head. "I am grateful for your kindness, but I have a city to save."

Larissa's father ran to a small box on top of the fireplace mantle, opened it, and removed a small coin. "Here is a quarter Cubit. It is all I have. Please, take this as payment for bringing my daughter back to me."

Dylan held his hands up in front of him, refusing the offer. "I cannot accept the last of your money."

The old farmer pressed the coin into Dylan's hand and rolled his fingers closed. "Yes. You can."

Dylan smiled at the old man. "Very well then."

He pocketed the coin and headed for the door. He turned around and addressed the group in the small farm cottage. "Thank you very much for your hospitality. In my travels, I have learned a bit of magic. In exchange for your generous gift," he patted the pocket he had placed the small coin in. "I will return to the corpse of the vile beast and perform a small ceremony that will protect your farm," he bowed to Larissa. "And your family from any future attacks."

The old farmer rushed forward, grabbed Dylan's hand, and kissed it repeatedly. "Thank you, thank you, thank you."

Dylan grimaced and pulled his hand away. "Yes, well, there is no greater cause than to keep the world safe from dragons. And it is my pleasure to do this for your family."

He opened the door and stepped out into the night, closing it behind him.

Suzy stood up from the table. "You two wait here. I'm going to follow him and see what he's up to."

Josh leaned in close. "What if he goes all the way back to the forest? How will you get back?"

She tilted her head down and looked at him like he was stupid.

His face shifted from confusion to understanding as he remembered that she could fly. "Oh right."

"If I'm not back by sunrise, head on to Silverrock. I'll find you there."

Once outside the cottage, and out of sight from anyone, Suzy lifted effortlessly into the air to follow Dylan, being certain to stay well behind him, and high enough that he wouldn't spot her in the sky if he looked back.

Within a couple of hours, he had made his way back to the forest in the center of the valley. She floated ahead and settled down in the top of a tree overlooking the still form of the dragon.

She waited and finally saw Dylan's torch light up the clearing in the middle of the woods as he stepped out from the dense forest and into the open area.

He walked up to the dragon lying on the ground and slapped it on the face. "I thought I told you to grab someone rich?"

Chapter 8

From the top of the tree, Suzy watched as the dragon rolled over onto his feet, dropped the arrow that he had held tucked tightly under his armpit, and sat next to Dylan.

Dylan set down the lamp and looked up at the dragon. Even sitting, the dragon was nearly as tall as a two story house, but he didn't look afraid. Instead, he looked disappointed.

"I know you have a brain in that massive skull of yours, no matter how tiny. When I tell you to grab someone, it's so that I can get paid a king's ransom for the safe return of your victim."

He pulled the quarter Cubit from his pocket and tossed it at the dragon. "This was everything they had. It's not enough to buy a loaf of bread."

The dragon reached out a claw and snatched the coin from the air with a swift motion. The dragon inspected it and then gave Dylan a sorrowful look.

"Don't give me that look. I tried to refuse it, but the old man insisted. I'm not looking to take everything away from someone; I just want a little more for me, that's all."

The dragon huffed loudly, plumes of smoke emanating from his nostrils, as he lowered his head. Dylan patted him on the side of his jaw. "I know. I know. But you're going to have to burn down a few buildings to make up for this mistake."

The dragon jerked his head away and looked angrily at Dylan.

Dylan held his hands out. "You messed up. What more can I say?"

Suzy was so enthralled watching Dylan talk to the dragon like a pet, she almost forgot she was on a branch at the top of a tree. She leaned forward and the branch creaked under her increased weight. Both Dylan's and the dragon's heads snapped up to look at her.

Dylan sneered and the dragon growled.

"Get her!" Dylan yelled.

The dragon's wings expanded outward and his powerful muscles pushed them toward the ground, lifting the dragon effortlessly into the air and headed straight for her.

She turned and shot into the sky. She had to warn everyone what was about to happen. But first, she had to get away.

She flew as fast as she could, the wind pulling her face back from the sheer speed she had achieved in a matter of seconds. But when she looked behind her, her heart sank.

The dragon was right behind her.

And he was getting closer.

Chapter 9

Suzy rolled sideways at the same moment she felt the wind from the powerful wings of the dragon. A claw brushed against her as she dropped away from his outstretched feet.

He had almost caught her that time.

She spiraled straight for the ground, not taking the risk to check behind her because that would only slow her down. She swooped in low over the tops of the trees. The moon sat high in the sky and cast a pallid glow over the forest, yet was still bright enough to show her the growing shadow of the dragon as it moved in behind her.

She felt the subtle shift of air to her left and rolled away from it, narrowly avoiding the claw that tried to snatch her out of mid air.

She dropped into the forest, darting around trees at incredible speed.

She glanced up.

The dragon was matching her every movement as he followed her above the treetops.

She slowed down and stopped in the middle of a thick part of the forest. The dragon was too big to reach her here.

She sat down on the cold, wet, ground and looked up through a small opening among the tops of the trees. The dragon circled around, tilting his head to cast an eye in her direction, letting her know that, while he couldn't get to her, he could still see her.

She couldn't stay still for very long. She must keep moving if she expected to get away.

She scanned the dark forest around her, looking for a thick section that would hide her from the dragon. She looked up, but he was gone. She strained to listen for the footfalls of Dylan in case he was sneaking up on her through the forest, but there was only silence from the trees around her.

They had to know right where she was. Why had they left her alone, especially after seeing that she could fly?

She stood up, ready to dart in any direction, when she smelled smoke.

She looked behind her and saw a wall of flame leap from the trees as the dragon swooped over them, igniting the forest.

She turned in the other direction, but the dragon had already lit that section of forest on fire. She turned again, but saw only flames.

She spun in a circle, checking the forest in every direction.

There was fire everywhere.

The small circle of safety she stood in was quickly shrinking as the fire spread to consume the forest around her.

The only way out, was up.

Right to where the dragon would be waiting for her.

Maybe she could outfly the dragon if she took off at a sharp angle rather than going straight up.

She shot out from the trees.

Behind her, the dragon screeched in delight as its prey was forcing back into the sky.

She had to get out of the valley and back to the city and warn the others.

She darted back and forth, trying to outmaneuver the dragon.

But he had been flying, and hunting, his entire life, while she had only just learned.

She willed herself to fly even faster,

focusing on being as straight as an arrow as she cut through the air.

Suddenly, her arms shot forward as her momentum ground to a halt.

She felt the tightening grip of scaly skin as the dragon closed his claws around her body.

She was jerked around as the dragon changed direction and dropped from the sky to land back in the same clearing where Dylan waited for them.

As soon as the dragon settled on the ground, he gripped Suzy tightly and held her out to show Dylan his catch.

Dylan walked up to Suzy and inspected her as she struggled helplessly against the strong hold of the dragon.

He smirked at her. "I don't want to harm you, little girl. But I also can't have you interfering with my work."

She struggled uselessly against the dragon's iron grip. "Let me go!"

He smiled at her. It was not a warm smile.

"I have a friend who will be very interested to know you can fly."

Chapter 10

Josh woke with the sun.

Sleeping in the digital world of Minecraft was very different from sleeping in the real world. For one, there was no sensation of time passing. From the moment he closed his eyes to when he awoke in the morning, it was like time had been compressed to the point of being non-existent. It was as if they had magically skipped the night to bring the arrival of morning mere moments after falling asleep.

Even though nobody really felt the passage of time while they slept in the real world, everyone still woke briefly a few times throughout the night, even if only a little bit, before falling asleep again as the brain cycled through the various stages of sleep.

While it was nice to not wake up in the middle of the night to the strange sounds of monsters under the bed, or in the closet, the thing he missed the most was dreaming.

There was none of that in the Minecraft world. He didn't know if this was something he would ever get used to.

As soon as the first light of the rising sun appeared, he opened his eyes slowly and became aware of the room Larissa had offered him and Andre for the night.

He glanced over at the other bed to see

Andre's eyes flutter and open. He sat up quickly and looked over at Josh.

"That is just the weirdest," Andre quipped. "Did you have any dreams while you slept?"

Josh sat up and shook his head. "Nope. I closed my eyes and suddenly it's morning."

Andre looked out the window. "That is just weird."

There was a faint knock at the door.

Josh cleared his throat. "Come in."

Larissa opened the door and poked her head in. "Father and I are taking our pickings to town. Would you like a ride?"

Andre hopped out of bed. "Did Suzy come back?"

She shook her head. "No. Is she alright?"

Josh tossed the blanket aside and stepped onto the cold floor. "I'm sure she's fine."

"Yeah, she said she'd meet us in town if she didn't make it back by the morning," Andre added as he smiled at Larissa. "We'd love a ride."

She smiled back at him. "I'll tell Father to wait then. Can you be ready in five minutes?"

Andre and Josh looked at each other before Josh looked back at her. "We're ready now."

"Excellent. I'll see you outside."

She disappeared and Andre grabbed Josh's arm before he walked out of the room. "Do you think something happened to her? I mean, why isn't she back?"

Josh shrugged. "I don't know. But she can fly, so I don't think Dylan would be able to catch her."

Andre nodded in agreement, and then a smile spread across his face. "You're probably right. She's waiting for us in town. And if I know her, she's probably already found all the best hotspots for us to enjoy once we get there."

Chapter 11

Suzy held onto the iron bars of her cage as it swung softly, suspended by a chain over a large pool of molten lava. She pressed her face against the bars, ignoring the searing heat that rose from below, and stared hard at Dylan. "You're not going to get away with this."

He laughed. "I'm not trying to get away with anything. I'm about to save a town from a dragon and get paid handsomely for my much needed and perfectly timed services."

She seethed inside as she tugged at the bars, but they didn't bend outward like she had seen in every cartoon. Why hadn't Notch also made the three of them stronger, instead of just giving them more health? She pulled with all her might, but it was no use.

She leaned against the bars again. "Someone's going to figure out that you and the dragon are working together."

He tilted his head to the side, as if he was contemplating her comment.

"Noooo, I don't think they will."

"Why not?"

"Nobody ever has before. You see, for every town I enter, I exit a hero to the people, with all the rewards that go with it."

"You're a villain."

"I'm neither. I'm just a businessman with a

unique service."

"You're a fraud."

"Not to the people I save. To them I am a friend."

"If it weren't for you, they wouldn't be attacked by a dragon in the first place."

He ignored her comment and his face grew distant as he let the memories from long ago overtake him. "I met someone when I was much younger, who gave me a gift. He told me that if I was willing to take the time to train a dragon, he would give me one.

"At first, I laughed at him. Dragon's were mythical creatures. They weren't real. And then he presented me this huge leathery egg.

He told me to keep it warm for thirty days, and then I would be the proud master of a dragon. The only one in the world."

Suzy clung to the bars on her swinging cage. "You can't be a dragon's master. What if it turns on you?"

He slipped a glowing purple crystal on a leather string necklace from around his neck. "As long as I have this, the dragon is bound to me. He will do whatever I ask."

A chill ran down Suzy's spine, despite the intense heat rising up from the pool of lava. "Who gave you this egg?"

Dylan smiled. "It was a gift from Him."

"Herobrine," she said aloud.

Dylan looked around him in a panic, as if Herobrine would magically appear at the mention of his name. He looked back at Suzy, his face looking more sinister than before with the reddish glow of lava. "Do not say His name."

Suzy smirked. "Why? Are you afraid of Him?"

"Just don't."

"Herobrine," Suzy said even louder.

Dylan put his hands over his ears. "Stop it!"

"Herobrine!" she shouted.

He rushed out of the cave as she continued to call out after him.

"Herobrine, Herobrine, Herobrine!"

Once he was gone, she inspected her cage more closely.

The bars were thick, and no matter how hard she pushed or pulled, they wouldn't budge. She was trapped.

She sat down on the floor of her cage and stuck her legs between the bars, hanging her feet out over the edge. The heat from the lava was too much, so she scooted back and sat in the center. While not completely comfortable, it was still the coolest spot inside the cage.

How was she going to get out of here and warn the town that the man who was about to protect them from a dragon attack was the one who caused the attack?

She looked around at the large cavern. Josh and Andre would eventually notice she never made it back to Silverrock and come looking for her.

But by then it would be too late.

If she planned to warn anyone before the city was destroyed, she had to get out of here herself.

Chapter 12

Josh and Andre hopped off the cart at the entrance to Silverrock.

Larissa leaned over the edge of the front seat of the large horse-drawn cart filled with baskets of strawberries.

"Are you sure you don't want us to take you into the city? Your friend might be waiting for you at the market. It's where all the action is."

Josh shook his head. "No thanks. The best place to wait for her is by the main gate where she can easily find us."

Larissa smiled. "Okay. Good luck."

She waved as her father snapped the reins and the horse pulled the cart away from them.

Josh turned to Andre. "You really think she'll be here?"

Andre pointed toward a growing crowd of onlookers just inside the main gate. "She has to be, look."

Josh looked where Andre was pointing. At the center of the large crowd was Dylan. Andre scanned the growing crowd around him.

"If she's following him, and he's here, then she should be somewhere nearby."

Josh checked everyone. "I don't see her."

Andre grabbed Josh's arm and pulled him

forward. "Maybe if we get closer..."

As they reached the edge of the crowd, they could hear Dylan speaking to everyone around him.

"The fortune teller told me to come to fair Silverrock and defend it from a dragon."

One man in the crowd had taken it upon himself to make fun of Dylan. "There's no such thing as dragons. So, good job. The town is saved."

Several people in the crowd laughed.

Dylan looked at the man. "How far would you say you have traveled sir?"

The man stopped laughing. "I've lived in Silverrock my entire life."

Dylan addressed the crowd as a whole. "Well I have been to the farthest corners of the world, and I know for a fact that dragons are real."

The man laughed. "And we are to take your word as truth?"

"No," Dylan replied. "I have already saved one of your own from being eaten by a dragon but yesterday. A young lady who picks strawberries in a field outside of town."

The man looked at him quizzically. "You mean Larissa?"

Dylan smiled. "Yes, Larissa was her name. She can vouch that dragons are not only real, but already close by. I can protect you from their impending attack, but I will need a personal item from everyone. A small coin or jewelry work the best. I need to be able to hold everything in my hands when I cast the protection spell. If even one person is left out, the entire city is still in danger."

The man began laughing. "Do you mean the same Larissa who says she used to play with tall black creatures with glowing eyes that could appear out of thin air?"

Josh and Andre looked at each other. The man had just described an Enderman.

The man continued while laughing harder. "The same Larissa who says her mother has been turned into a zombie?"

The entire crowd was laughing uncontrollably now.

The man's face turned multiple shades of purple as he gasped for air while laughing even harder. "The same Larissa who said that the world, and everything and everyone in it, didn't really exist?"

Josh and Andre backed away from the crowd and ducked into a side alley.

Andre glanced around, to make sure no one was close enough to hear them. "Did you hear that?"

Josh nodded. "Herobrine has definitely been through here."

Andre agreed with a nod and peeked

around the corner to scan the dwindling crowd. "Where's Suzy?"

Josh shrugged his shoulders. "What if she's still following him but staying out of sight? If we stay close, maybe she will see us and come out of hiding."

They stepped back out of the alley and blended in with the crowd, which was getting harder as more people moved away to return to their daily chores.

Dylan kept grabbing at people as they tried to leave. "Mark my words, this town is in danger. Sir, please. Madame?"

The crowd dispersed leaving Josh and Andre standing alone on the cobblestone street, looking at Dylan, who let out a big sigh. He took a deep breath and smiled at the boys.

"You guys both saw the dragon that I killed. The rest of the brood will come here looking for vengeance. Why didn't you speak up?"

Josh glanced over at Andre, silencing him. "We really don't want to get involved in local politics."

Dylan frowned. "What politics? If I can't get everyone in this city to give me something small and personal, they will all be killed."

Andre stepped forward. "Something small, like a ring or bracelet?"

Dylan nodded, smiling wide. "Anything

really. Money is the easiest personal item that I can use to cast a protection spell. I only need it to keep everyone safe."

Josh stepped forward, pulling Andre back with an outstretched arm. "Where's Suzy?"

Dylan looked around. "Who?"

"The girl that was with us last night."

"Why would I know where she is?"

Andre moved in close and glared at him. "She never came back. And she was following you."

Dylan looked away. "I don't have time for this. I have a town to save."

Dylan started walking away when Josh got in his way. "What did you do with her?"

"I didn't do anything. I never saw her after I left last night. Now, if you'll excuse me."

Josh stepped in his way again. "Where is she?"

"I don't know kid. And if you don't get out of my way, I'll..."

Josh took a step closer to him. "You'll what?"

They stood, facing each other, without moving.

A soft voice from down the street called out to them. "I knew I'd find you here."

They looked and saw Larissa smiling at them as she hurried down the street in their direction, talking loudly for everyone around to hear. "I wanted to thank you properly for saving my life yesterday."

Once she got close, she gave Dylan a big hug.

Josh was still close enough to hear her whisper into Dylan's ear.

"If you don't leave, and take your dragon with you, I will make sure that this town is the last place you will ever visit."

Dylan stiffened in her embrace. She held him out at arm's length while still gripping his shoulders in each hand. She smiled at him. "Do we understand one another?"

His forehead crinkled in confusion. "I am here to save the town."

"I know what you told me and my father last night. And because he doesn't know about the colony, I didn't say anything. But I knew you would be here this morning, running your little scam."

"I don't know what you are talking about?"

Her smile faded. "You know exactly what I am talking about. And if you don't move on and take your show someplace else, I will stop you."

He shook himself out of her grip. "Even if what you were implying was even remotely true, you could never stop me."

She smiled again. "Oh, can't I?"

He stuck out his chin defiantly. "No, you

can't."

"Maybe I can't." She tugged at a string around her neck and produced a red crystal tied to the end of it. "But my dragon can."

Chapter 13

Josh and Andre looked at each other. Andre leaned close and whispered to Josh. "Did she just say she had a dragon?"

Josh nodded his head.

Rather than look frightened, Dylan laughed. "You wish me to believe you control a dragon?"

She shoved the crystal in his face. "Do not test me!"

He snatched the crystal out of her hand, the string snapping in half as he pulled the crystal from around her neck. He held it up to inspect it in the sunlight. "If you knew anything about how to control a dragon, you would know that this is the wrong color."

She massaged her neck where the string had left a red mark before snapping in half. "And how would you know?"

He slipped out a purple glowing crystal attached to a necklace around his own neck. "Because little girl, you need one that looks like this."

She grabbed the glowing crystal, the necklace snapping loudly as pulled tight around his neck. She sliced the necklace in two with a dagger that appeared in her hand and then darted off into the city with her prize, Dylan hot on her heels yelling after her.

"Give that back!"

Chapter 14

Andre gasped for air loudly next to Josh as they ran as fast as they could to keep up with Dylan and Larissa. "Now…" He took in a quick breath. "Would have been a good time…" He sucked in another big breath. "To know how to fly."

Josh was breathing just as heavily, trying to catch his own breath. "As soon as we find her, we'll get her to teach us."

"You still think Dylan knows where she is?"

"I think that she saw him controlling the dragon last night and he did something to her."

"Makes sense. But how do we get him to tell us?"

Josh surged faster. "We have to catch him first."

They sped around a corner and collided with a hay cart, both of them bouncing off the side of the cart and sprawling on the ground. The man shoveling hay out of the cart looked down at them. "Easy boys. What's your big hurry?"

Josh quickly stood up and helped Andre to his feet. He looked around, but Dylan was nowhere to be seen. Andre was also glancing around in all directions. "Which way did they go?"

Josh scanned the crowded marketplace and checked every exit. He didn't see Dylan or Larissa.

They were both gone.

Andre grabbed his shoulders. "Where did they go?"

Josh looked him in the eye. "I don't know."

"What do we do?"

Andre's question probed right to the heart of the matter. Suzy was missing, and only Dylan could tell them where she was.

If this world was supposed to be a mirror of the real world, there shouldn't be any dragons in it. But they had all seen the dragon.

Come to think of it, there were many things they had seen that shouldn't have been here at all.

Herobrine was not only alive and well in this world, he was changing it.

But what was he changing it for? What did he get out of bringing Creepers, zombies, and dragons to this world?

Some stupid thrill? Just because he could?

That didn't make sense. There had to be some reason that He was creating the creatures that plagued the players in the regular game. Creatures that shouldn't exist in this real-world simulation.

Josh dug into his bag and pulled out the

map. Andre looked at him with a confused expression. "What are you doing? The map's not going to tell us which way they went."

Josh unfolded the map and laid it out on the edge of the hay cart. "Quiet and let me think."

Andre stood next to him. "What are..."

"Shush!"

Josh studied the map, noting the areas marked as the access points to the internet from this world. According to the briefing Notch gave them before coming into this world, the access points were strongholds that were heavily defended. Nobody could just walk right in and take it without a fight.

They were close to one of them. And Herobrine had been very active in the towns all around it.

That is what Herobrine had been doing for the past hundred years.

He was building an army capable of attacking an access point.

But you couldn't hide an army of any size without someone noticing. Unless, you created a place that nobody was willing to go. A place where you could hide a large army and nobody would find out.

He looked over at the hay cart driver. "Excuse me?"

The driver looked down at him and

stopped shoveling hay into a pile on the side of the road. "Yes?"

"Is there a place around here that is forbidden?"

The man's brow furrowed. "Now why would you ask such a question?"

Andre stood up straighter. "Just answer him."

The man leaned on his pitchfork. "No. I won't be party to young boys getting into trouble."

Andre stepped forward, about to say something, when Josh placed a hand on his shoulder and stopped him. "Let me handle this Andre."

He smiled at the man. "We aren't looking to get into any trouble. We are planning out our journey and need to know what to stay away from, that's all."

The man removed his hat and wiped the sweat from the back of his neck with a dingy scrap of cloth. "Well, in that case, you will want to steer clear of the temple."

"What temple?"

"I wasn't around back then, but they say it was built in a single night nearly fifty years ago. I went to check it out when I first heard about it, but it looked like an old temple to me. It didn't look magical, or haunted. Certainly not worthy of the stories told about it."

"Then why is it forbidden to go there?"

"The place sits directly over the lava pits. Nobody goes anywhere near it for fear that the ground will crumble away and expose the lava."

"Can you show me the area on my map so we can avoid it?"

"Sure."

The man circled a blank area on the map with his finger. "This whole area has lava underneath it. It's best if you stick to the main roads on your way to the next town."

Josh folded up the map and thanked the man.

He stuffed the map into his bag as he
hurried away from the hay cart.

Andre ran to catch up to him. "Where are
we going?"

Josh smiled as he ran.

"I think I know where Suzy is."

Chapter 15

Larissa ducked beneath a cart in the center of the market and held a hand over her mouth to quiet her heavy breathing.

Dylan stopped in front of the cart and glanced in every direction before picking one and running off into the crowded city.

Larissa waited several minutes before climbing out from under the cart and running in the opposite direction.

She didn't stop until she had made it to the edge of the city. She glanced at the glowing purple crystal in her hand. With this, she would be able to find her mother and rescue her.

Maybe there would even be enough magic left in the crystal to cure her mother from the disease that had changed her.

She held the crystal aloft and watched as the dragon swooped in low toward where she stood waiting.

Chapter 16

Suzy raised herself into the air inside the cage. She pressed herself against the roof of the cage and lifted it higher until it was touching the ceiling of the massive underground chamber.

She looked down at the pool of lava below. She figured she had just enough time, and health, to crash the cage into the lava below, let the heat from the lava melt the bars, and escape before the heat from the lava killed her too.

She took three deep breaths and flew down as fast as she could, pushing the cage down with her. The chain extended all the way, snapped tight with a metallic twang, but refused to break.

She picked herself up from the floor of the cage and inspected the bruises all over her body from having tried this same maneuver several times.

A voice echoed up to her from the entrance to the underground cavern.

"That chain is made from tempered obsidian. Nothing can break it. At least, nothing you have access to."

She looked over at the source of the voice and stared directly into a pair of bright glowing eyes.

"Herobrine," she whispered to herself.

His face changed to one of slight amusement. "You are the first person I have met to actually have me at a disadvantage. You obviously know who I am, but, I don't know who you are."

He walked up to the edge of the lava pit and stared up at her.

"But we have plenty of time to remedy that. Don't we?"

Find out what happens to Josh and Andre.

Collect the whole series!

Other Books by the Author

A is for Apprentice (Fantasy)

Oliver Twist: Victorian Vampire (Fantasy-Horror)

A Tale of Two Cities with Dragons (Fantasy)

Shade Infinity (Thriller)

Peacekeepers X-Alpha Series (Thriller)
> **Inherit the Throne**
> **The Warrior's Code**

Steampunk OZ Series (Science Fiction Novellas)
> **Forgotten Girl**
> **The Legacy's World**
> **Emerald Shadow**
> **The Future's Destiny**
> **The Dangerous Captive**
> **Missing Legacy**
> **Shadow of History**
> **The Edge of the Hunter**

Jason and the Chrononauts (Kid's Adventure Series)
> **The Chronicle of Stone**
> **The Winter's Sun**
> **The Gateway's Mirror**
> **The Forgotten Oracle**
> **The Prophecy's Touch**
> **The Dawn Legend**

Be the first to know about Steve DeWinter's next book. Follow the URL below to subscribe for free today!

http://bit.ly/BookReleaseBulletin

CPSIA information can be obtained
at www.ICGtesting.com
Printed in the USA
LVOW10s1528081116

512137LV00002B/568/P